WIMEE'S WORDS

WIMEE CREATES
with Vehicles and Colors

WRITTEN BY
STEPHANIE KAMMERAAD

CREATED BY
MICHAEL HYACINTHE AND **KEVIN KAMMERAAD**

ZONDER**kidz**

Wimee picks words,
he finds a rhyme,
he plays with them,
and then with time ...
he creates an image.

van   can

A red van vanished under the orange can.

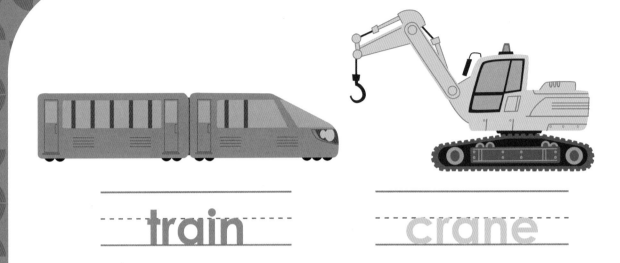

train crane

An orange train trekked below the yellow crane.

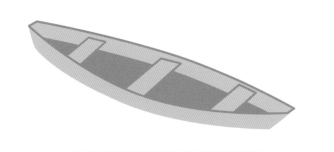

canoe

kazoo

A yellow canoe curved around the green kazoo.

wagon

dragon

A green wagon wheeled behind the blue dragon.

jet

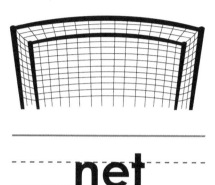

net

A blue jet journeyed above the purple net.

balloon

baboon

A purple balloon bumped against the red baboon.

rocket

pocket

A red rocket raced into the orange pocket.

plow

cow

An orange plow plodded beside the yellow cow.

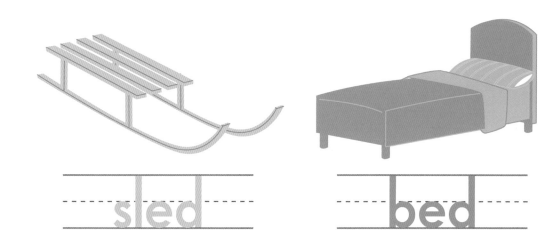

sled   bed

A yellow sled slid

across the green bed.

boat

goat

A green boat balanced on the blue goat.

jeep

sheep

A blue jeep jumped over the purple sheep.

skate

gate

A purple skate skidded through the red gate.

Wimee creates
throughout each day
by using words
to sing and play.

You can do the same things too.
Go make things that are from you!

Notes to educators and parents:

Wimee's Words: *Wimee Creates with Vehicles and Colors* is a simple book with lots of opportunities for discussion, games, and interactivity! Here are some ideas for how you can use this book to continue learning and inspiring creativity.

- Each of Wimee's sentences has a subject noun with the same beginning sound as the verb that follows it: alliteration (e.g. van vanished, train trekked). Encourage your children to come up with other words that have the same beginning sounds.

- Each of Wimee's sentences contain a strong action verb. Try acting them out with your children!

- There are twelve different prepositions in the book (e.g., under, across, and on). Each of these location words can be acted out with children using objects in their environment. For example, put a book *under* a table or a cup *on* a shelf.

- Each line of the book is written in rhyme. On subsequent readings, don't say the object word (e.g., kazoo, dragon, and sheep) aloud. Then have your children guess it and "read" the book with you. Encourage them to think of even more rhyming words!

- The subject of each sentence is described using the color of the object from the previous sentence. For example, "The red van vanished under the orange can" is followed by "The orange train trekked below the yellow crane." As children notice the pattern, ask them to predict what color is coming next.

- Talk about the objects on each page in relation to their color (For example, ask what color the van is; have the child point to the red van; point to all the words that are in red; ask if anything else on the page is red). Encourage them to talk about other things they know of that are red. Explore other colors by asking what others besides red they see on the pages or be specific and ask if they see a certain color, such as purple.

- Explore the endpapers of the book with your children. Point to a word and have them find the rhyme. For the words that don't have a rhyme on the page, point to the empty spot and say: What rhyming word could be put there?

- Look at just the illustrations. Ask:
    —What do you see? What is happening in the image?
    —I wonder what happened just before?
    —I wonder what might happen next?

- Listen to and download the accompanying song on www.wimee.tv.

- Wimee has his own TV show: *Wimee's Words!* Watch and participate live every week on wimee.tv or search for Wimee on pbs.org to watch previous episodes.

For even more fun with Wimee and words, check out the Wimage app (free in the App store)! Wimage helps children explore their creativity and enhances their storytelling by changing words into images. Kids type or say a word into the app and icons of that word appear. The image can change size, color, placement, and more to create their very own story or wimage.

ZONDERKIDZ

Wimee Creates with Vehicles and Colors
Copyright © 2023 by Wimage, LLC
Illustrations © 2023 by Wimage, LLC

Requests for information should be addressed to:

Zonderkidz, 3900 Sparks Drive, Grand Rapids, Michigan 49546

Hardcover ISBN 978-0-310-15358-0
Ebook ISBN 978-0-310-15360-3

Zondervan titles may be purchased in bulk for educational, business, fundraising, or sales promotional use.
For information, please email SpecialMarkets@Zondervan.com.

Zonderkidz is a trademark of Zondervan.

Illustrations: Mattia Cerato
Editor: Katherine Jacobs
Design and art direction: Cindy Davis

Printed in India

_____

23 24 25 26 27 28 / REP/ 14 13 12 11 10 9 8 7 6 5 4 3 2 1

WIMEE'S WORDS